SOUNDS OF A
SUMMER NIGHT

by
May Garelick

illustrations by
Candace Whitman

MONDO

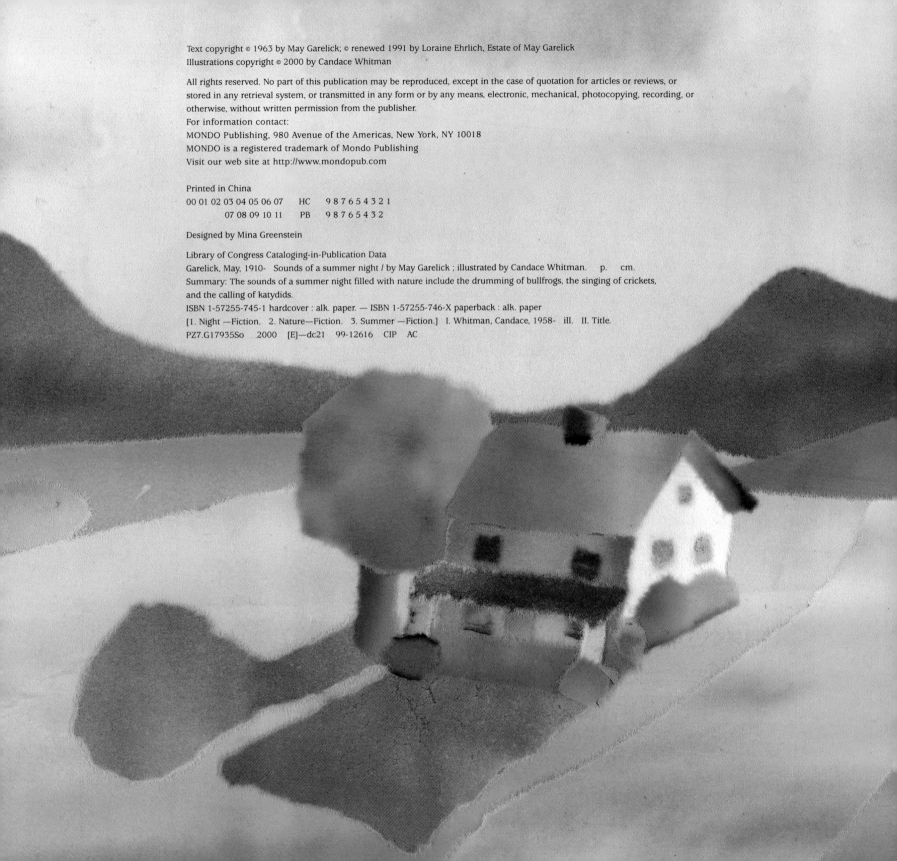

For information contact:
MONDO Publishing, 980 Avenue of the Americas, New York, NY 10018
MONDO is a registered trademark of Mondo Publishing
Visit our web site at http://www.mondopub.com

Printed in China
00 01 02 03 04 05 06 07   HC   9 8 7 6 5 4 3 2 1
        07 08 09 10 11   PB   9 8 7 6 5 4 3 2

Designed by Mina Greenstein

Library of Congress Cataloging-in-Publication Data
Garelick, May, 1910- Sounds of a summer night / by May Garelick ; illustrated by Candace Whitman.   p.   cm.
Summary: The sounds of a summer night filled with nature include the drumming of bullfrogs, the singing of crickets,
and the calling of katydids.
ISBN 1-57255-745-1 hardcover : alk. paper. — ISBN 1-57255-746-X paperback : alk. paper
[1. Night —Fiction. 2. Nature—Fiction. 3. Summer —Fiction.] I. Whitman, Candace, 1958- ill. II. Title.
PZ7.G17935So   2000   [E]—dc21   99-12616   CIP   AC

For Ray and Mike—M.G.

With memories of Jamesport—C.W

You lie in bed, not asleep.
Even the birds are not asleep.
Fee-bee Fee-bee Bob-o-link
Cheep.

A soft breeze stirs
the leaves in the trees—
soft rustle of leaves.

Slowly, the sun goes down,
down behind the mountain,
down.

Streaks of pink
light up the sky,
and pink is the water
in the pond below.

No sound
but the quiet lapping of the water,
the soft rustle of leaves.

Gone is the pink
from the sky,
from the water.
Gone is the last light of day.

In the dim half-light
comes the signal of night—
the voice of a swallow.

Night has come.

Bullfrogs drum.
D-d-dum. D-d-dum.
Crickets sing
the cricket song.
Chirp-chirp-chirp-chirp-chirp.
Katydids call the Katydid call.
Katydid Katydid Katy-did-did-did.

What did Katy do?
Katydid Katydid
Katy-did-did-did.

And without a sound
as it flickers by,
goes the silent firefly.
Spark
     flicker
         glow
            glitter.
How many fireflies glittering by
blink their lights in a summer night?

One, two, three, four?

More, more, more, and more.

Seven, eleven, forty-seven?

Many, many, many more.

Voices.
Grownups talking
in their nighttime voices.

Footsteps coming into the house.

Tick Tock.
The clock ticking by the door
sounds louder than before—
louder than the voices,
clearer than the footsteps.

Tick tock
tick
tock.

Tick tock
　　drum frog
　　　　tick tock
　　　　　　bullfrog
　　　　　　　　leap frog
　　　　　　　　　　still frog
　　　　　　　　　　　　bullfrog
　　　　　　　　　　　　　did.

Katy-did.
Did what?
Didn't did.
Grum did.
Frog-a-log
Katy tock.
Wicked cricket?

No, no, not so,
gentle, slow,
low creep,
soft sleep,
sleepy, sleepy,
sleep.

Thump!
Pounce! Leap! Bounce!
Listen.
It must be the squirrel
that pounces across the roof
every morning.

Morning?

Is it morning?
Fee-bee Fee-bee
Caw Caw Caw
and the sound of the tractor
coming up the road.

Crows do not caw in the night.
Birds do not sing.
No tractor comes up the road
at night.
It must be morning.

A humming, buzzing, stirring
summer morning.